HURRY DOWN TO
DERRY FAIR

For Ann Angel, Sharon Addy, JoAnn Macken, Gretchen Mayo
and Lisa Moser – in friendship ~ D. C.

For Isaac Jude ~ G. T.

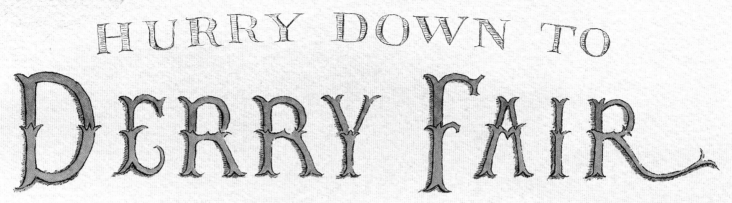

HURRY DOWN TO DERRY FAIR

DORI CHACONAS

ILLUSTRATED BY GILLIAN TYLER

WALKER BOOKS

AND SUBSIDIARIES

LONDON · BOSTON · SYDNEY · AUCKLAND

GIANT SWING

"Hurry, Mummy! Please, let's go!
Let's go to Derry Fair!
I want to ride the giant swing
That flies high
in the air!"

"Billy Brown, don't hurry so!
I'm making lemon pies.
I'm going to take them to the fair.
I hope they win a prize!"

"I'll whisk the eggs so we can go!

Please hurry, Mummy! Don't be slow!"

Whap! Crack!
Plop-plop-plop!

Whisk a little! Whisk a lot!

Whisk those eggs as light as air.

Mummy sifts while Billy whisks.

Then off they'll go to Derry Fair!

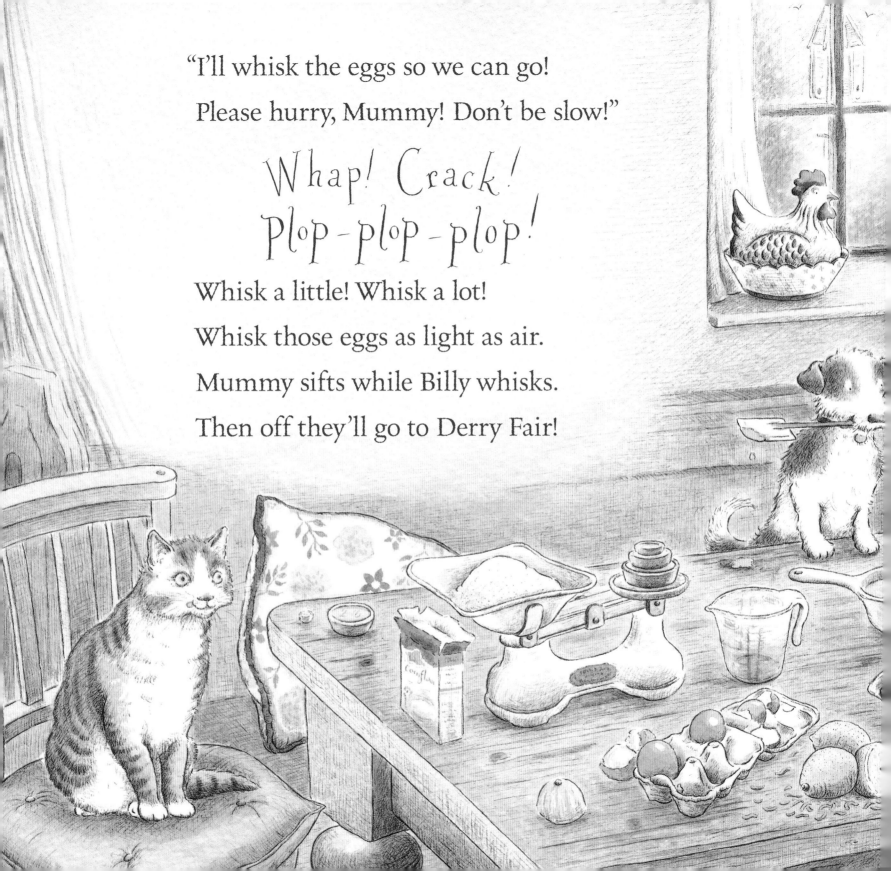

"Hurry, Daddy! Please! It's time
To walk to Derry Fair.
The rabbits, chickens, woolly sheep
And horses
        will be there!"

"Billy Brown, don't worry so!
I need to chop this wood.
I'm going to sell it at the fair.
Please help me
    if you could."

"I'll help you stack so we can go!

Please hurry, Daddy! Don't be slow!"

Whack! Smack!
Stack-stack-stack!

Stack a little! Stack a lot!

Wood chips in a flying flurry.

Whack'em, smack'em, stack'em high!

Almost finished!

Hurry! Hurry!

"Sister Lucy, time to go!

If we don't get there soon,

We'll miss the cherry candy floss

And red hot

air balloon!"

"Brother Bill, don't worry so!

My animals need brushing.

I'm going to show them at the fair.

Please help me!

Stop your rushing!"

"Lucy, you are much too slow!
We're going to miss the talent show!"

*Swish! Swash!
Swoosh – swoosh – swoosh!*

Brush a little! Brush a lot!
Piggy, puppy, old grey goosey.
Fur and feathers fly about
While Billy hurries Sister Lucy.

"Grandma Patty! Time to go!

The Derry fair won't wait!

We're going to miss the Ferris wheel!"

"You're right," she said.
"It's late!"

"So Billy Brown,

     please fetch your coins,

Then meet me at the door.

I'm taking you to Derry Fair!

You won't wait any more!"

"We're leaving now!" calls Grandma Patty.
"See you later, Mummy, Daddy!
Sister Lucy, you take care..."

Mummy bundles up the pies
And slips them in a sack.

Daddy bundles up the wood
And slings it on his back.

Lucy bundles up her pets
And hurries to the gate.

They rush and tumble
down the walk...

Billy!
Grandma!
Wait!

Mummy, Daddy, Sister Lucy,

Grandma, piggy, puppy, goosey,

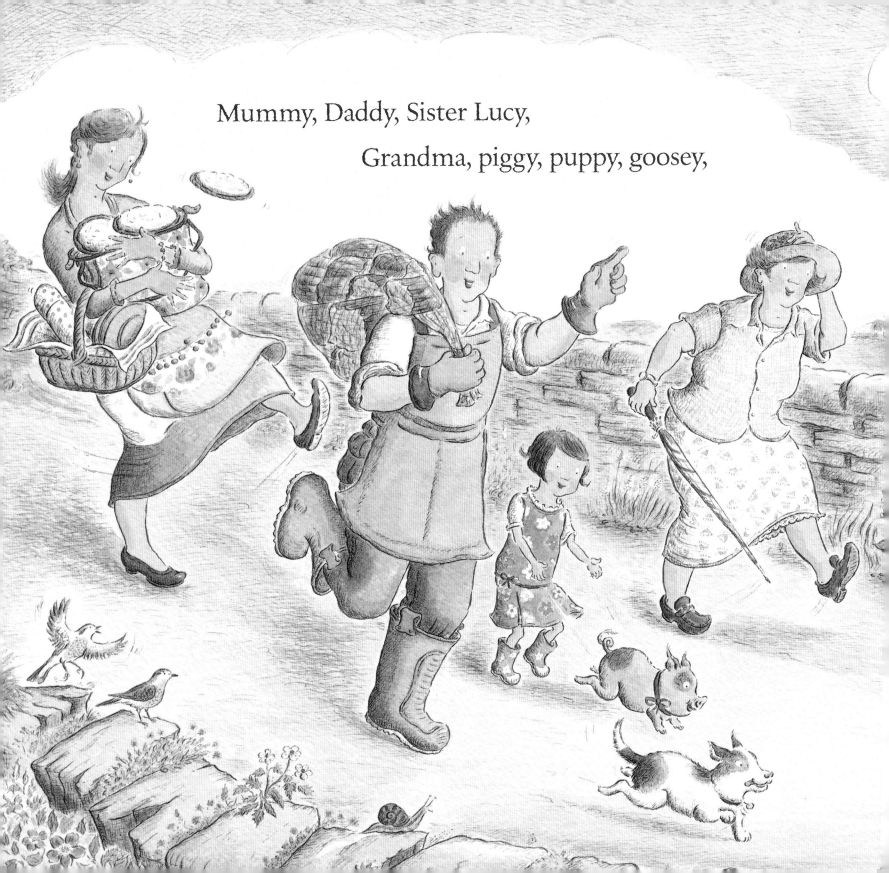

Running down the road to town

To see the fair with Billy Brown!

First published 2011 by Walker Books Ltd, 87 Vauxhall Walk, London SE11 5HJ • 2 4 6 8 10 9 7 5 3 1 • Text © 2011 Dori Chaconas • Illustrations © 2011 Gillian Tyler • The right of Dori Chaconas and Gillian Tyler to be identified as author and illustrator respectively of this work has been asserted by them in accordance with the Copyright, Designs and Patents Act 1988 • This book has been typeset in Quercus • Printed in China • All rights reserved. No part of this book may be reproduced, transmitted or stored in an information retrieval system in any form or by any means, graphic, electronic or mechanical, including photocopying, taping and recording, without prior written permission from the publisher. • British Library Cataloguing in Publication Data: a catalogue record for this book is available from the British Library. • ISBN 978-1-4063-0379-7 • www.walker.co.uk